Death Sentence

Leo P. Kelley

 CHILDRENS PRESS, CHICAGO

The SPACE POLICE™ Series

Prison Satellite	Backward in Time
Worlds Apart	Sunworld
Earth Two	Death Sentence

Childrens Press Edition
Editorial Director: Robert G. Bander
Managing Designer: Kauthar Hawkins
Cover and interior illustrator: Steven Hofheimer

ISBN 0–516–02232–6

Library of Congress Catalog Card Number: 79-51081

Printed in the United States of America.

1.9   8   7   6   5   4   3   2   1

CONTENTS

WORKERS IN THE BLUE GAS

It had been a dead world, covered with a strange blue gas. Then the first humans had come to it from Earth and changed it into a world they could live in. The Earth people had made big glass domes to live in. They had made long tunnels so they could walk from dome to dome. They had filled the domes and tunnels with air. They called their dome world New Earth.

The people lived inside the domes. No human could go outside without a spacesuit. That was because of the blue gas. It didn't kill the humans. But it made them think they saw things that were not really there. The gas worked on people's minds. It made their thoughts take real shape and appear before them.

But life inside the domes was good. The people were happy. They lived in small, beautiful houses. They kept in touch with Earth and many other worlds in space. They had many interesting things to do when they weren't working.

Most of the people of New Earth worked in the fields outside the domes. They cared for the yellow plants that grew there. These plants weren't used for food. All of the food on New Earth grew in water inside the domes. The yellow plants were made into a special kind of medicine. The medicine was very strong. It helped many sick people to get well. They always got better after they took the medicine. The people of New Earth kept some of the medicine to make their own people better. They sold the rest to Earth and many other worlds.

One day, some of the people who lived on New Earth were getting ready to go out into the fields. One of the people was a young man named Michael. Another was a young woman named Tanya. Michael and Tanya had been born on New Earth. They had lived there all their lives. They were very much in love and planned to get married soon. After they were married they planned to visit Earth.

Michael and Tanya talked about Earth as they put on their spacesuits to go outside. Soon they were both ready to leave the dome. They walked to the air lock with the rest of the people who were going to work in the fields. When everyone was inside the air lock, a glass door behind them closed. Then a large door in front of them opened. The strange blue gas came into the air lock. But it didn't hurt the people because they were all wearing spacesuits.

Everyone left the air lock. The door closed behind them. Then the blue gas was taken out of the air lock. Air took its place.

Tanya and Michael walked with the rest of the people to the fields. Soon the two found a place where the plants looked ready to be picked. They began to work side by side. Before long they had pulled up many plants.

Tanya kept picking plants. Michael stopped to put the plants they had already picked into one of the big bags he had brought with him. As he worked he thought about how his life would soon change. He would be living with Tanya. They would be very happy. And they would soon take their trip to Earth.

Michael had seen pictures of Earth. But he had never seen Earth itself. He was looking forward to it. It was the world where his parents had been born. That fact made Earth seem very real to him.

Michael's bag was soon full of plants. He tied it up. Then he started to fill another bag. As he did the blue gas got very thick around him. He couldn't see Tanya.

He dropped his bag. He began to move through the blue gas trying to find her. He knew it was silly but he felt afraid. Wild thoughts raced through his mind. What if he had lost Tanya? What if her spacesuit wasn't working right? What if a lion or a tiger or a giant bird had caught her? Even though Michael knew those animals lived only on Earth, he was still afraid.

He moved on through the thick blue gas. He called out, "Tanya!" And again, "Tanya!"

"Watch out!"

It was Tanya's voice. Then Michael saw her. She was right in front of him. In fact he had stepped on her foot as he moved through the blue gas.

She asked him, "What's the matter?"

"Nothing," he answered. "I was just wondering where you were. I couldn't see you."

"Did you think I had run out on you?" Tanya had a smile on her face.

"I hope you never do," Michael said. "Come on over this way. My bag is there."

Tanya walked with him to the spot where the half-filled bag lay. Then she began to pull up more plants. Michael stuffed them into his bag. Soon it was filled. Before their time in the fields was over they had filled three more bags.

Tanya and Michael walked with the other people who were leaving the fields. Everyone carried bags full of plants. They headed for the air lock and home.

It didn't take them long to reach the air lock. Tanya reached out to open the door. But it wouldn't open. She tried a second time. It stayed closed. She looked at Michael.

"Let me try," he said. But he couldn't open the door either. Several other people tried. Finally a woman pushed it open by pressing the top and bottom at the same time. The door closed behind them.

Everyone waited until the blue gas that had come into the air lock with them was taken out. When it was gone, air took its place. Then the people took off their spacesuits. A man started to open the door that led into the dome. It wouldn't open. Several people tried very hard to open it. But none of them could do it.

They were still trying to open the door when the door behind them opened by itself. Blue gas rushed in. A woman let out a cry when she saw what had happened. A man grabbed the door and tried to close it. But he couldn't make it move.

Michael kicked at the air lock's door—the one that led into the dome. It stayed closed. Then he heard Tanya call his name. He turned around. A big lion was coming toward Tanya through the blue gas.

Tanya ran to Michael. They both tried to push open the locked door. Suddenly the lion was joined by a tiger. Then a giant bird flew down out of the sky. A woman screamed. Everyone pushed and cried as they tried to open the door into the dome.

Then the lion jumped. Michael tried to push Tanya out of its way. But it landed on both of them.

"Tanya!" Michael shouted at the top of his voice as he tried to fight off the lion. But she didn't answer him. She lay on the ground at his feet. Her eyes were closed. The tiger stood over her. Its yellow eyes were the last thing Michael saw before everything around him went black.

A CALL FOR HELP

A Space Police ship flew high above New Earth. In front of it was a much bigger ship with *C-2* painted on its side. The bigger ship shot jets of red fire at the police ship. The police ship fired back.

Inside the police ship, Officer Ted Prentiss watched the control board in front of him. He was tracking the big ship. He rubbed his face with his right hand. The fingers of his left hand drummed on the control board. Suddenly he turned around and gave orders to the other police officers on his ship.

He shouted through his ship's speakers, "C-2 is going to get away from us! Fire the big guns!"

Jets of many colors shot out into space. Some hit ship C-2. Some didn't. The ship flew on.

Ted told one of the officers, "Order the people on board C-2 to give up!" He heard the woman give the order. He also heard the answer that came back from the other ship:

"We'll never give up!"

Ted knew what he had to do. Twice before he had blown up ships in space. He hadn't liked doing it. But he was about to do it again. It was the only way to stop ship C-2.

And it had to be stopped. It was heading for the spaceship Campo, where many humans lived. The people on board C-2 had once lived on the spaceship Campo. But they had left it when they couldn't run things their own way. Now they were planning to blow up Campo and kill all the people on it.

Ted ordered, "We'll fire all our guns at once! Try to hit the nose of the ship. Ready . . . *fire!*"

All the guns on the police ship fired together. Their shots hit the nose of the other ship. It blew up in a big white fire.

"That's the end of them." An officer passed the message on over the police ship's speakers. Ted was glad it was over. But he couldn't help feeling sorry for the men and women who had just died on C-2. Ted wished they could have found a way to live together in peace with the people who had once been their friends. They hadn't been able to. Now they were all dead.

Ted looked out the window in front of him. Pieces of C-2 floated in space. He looked away from the window. Just then a call came over his speaker.

"This is Fleet Commander calling Officer Prentiss on Fleet Ship Four. Do you read me, Prentiss? Over."

Ted answered her call. "This is Fleet Ship Four. Officer Prentiss speaking. Over."

"We've just had a call from New Earth, Prentiss," the fleet commander said. "They've got trouble on their world. They asked for help. They said they need it fast. I want you to go to New Earth at once. See what's wrong there and do what you can about it. You can join your ship again when you've cleared up the trouble on New Earth."

"I don't want to go to New Earth," Ted said. He had always liked his work on the ship better than work on any of the worlds. He was sure the problem on New Earth wouldn't be interesting. He drummed his fingers on the control board. "I'm needed here on Fleet Ship Four," he said.

"Right now you're needed on New Earth, Prentiss," the fleet commander said.

"Maybe there's a ship closer to New Earth than we are," Ted said. "Someone from that ship could go."

"Prentiss, I've given you an order. Don't make me give it again. Do you understand?"

"Yes," Ted answered. "But my job here on Fleet Ship Four is important."

"All police work is important, Prentiss," barked the fleet commander. "And I'll decide where you do that work."

"I'll leave for New Earth right away," Ted said. "Over and out."

He left the control board. He went to the ship's dock. He put on his spacesuit. Then he got one of the small space capsules ready to fly.

Soon Ted got into the capsule. He set its

controls so that it would take him to New Earth. Then he fired the capsule. It shot out of the police ship's dock into space. It shot past stars and suns as it made its way toward New Earth.

When it landed on New Earth, Ted got out. He found himself in a field of yellow plants. There were no people to be seen. A blue gas floated all around him. He started toward the nearest dome. When he reached it he found its air lock and went inside. Then he came out into the world under the dome.

He took off his spacesuit and left it beside the air lock. A few people nearby saw that he was a Space Police officer. They ran toward him. All of them began to talk at once.

Ted couldn't understand what they were saying. He pointed to a man and asked him to explain what the trouble was. He told the other people to let the man speak.

The man said, "A lot of our people were killed in one of our air locks."

Ted asked, "Who killed them?"

"A lion," said a woman.

"A tiger and a big bird," said another woman.

Ted held up his hand. "One person speaks at a time. Let this man tell me what happened."

The man said, "It's true. A lion and a tiger and a giant bird killed our people as they were coming in from the fields."

"Where's the air lock where this happened?" Ted asked.

The man said it was in the next dome. Ted asked the man to take him there. They left the dome and went through a tunnel to the next dome.

The man took Ted to the air lock in that dome. He pointed through the air lock's glass door. "The people who died are still inside," he said. "Only one person in the air lock lived—a little boy. He was hidden from the animals under a fallen body. He told us what had happened."

Ted looked at the dead people on the ground. There were a lot of them. But there was no lion or tiger or bird.

"None of these people have any marks on them," he said to the man at his side. "But you said they were killed by wild animals."

"They were," the man said. Then he explained to Ted about the blue gas that covered

New Earth outside the domes. He told Ted that it did strange things to people's minds. It made their thoughts become real. He ended by saying, "These people saw a lion. They also saw a tiger and a bird. The animals and bird weren't real, of course. But the blue gas made the people believe they were."

"I get it," Ted said. "These people thought that they saw two wild animals and a bird. And because they did the people were scared to death by them."

"That's right," said the man. "They were scared to death—not clawed to death."

"Then I'm not sure why you called the Space Police," Ted said. "These people are dead. But no one killed them. So there's no one for me to track down."

"We know that," the man said. "But we called you because we can't get that air lock to work. We don't know how to fix the doors. You see, the people in the air lock were trying to get into the dome. But they couldn't because the inside air lock door wouldn't open. Then the blue gas came in the open door. And they all died."

Ted felt his face grow stiff. It always did when he was getting mad. He said, "Do you mean to tell me that you called the Space Police so an officer would come here to fix a broken air lock?"

"Oh, no," the man said. "Not that. You don't understand."

"That's right," Ted said. "I don't understand. So will you please tell me why you wanted me here? I have a very important job on my ship. I don't want to waste my time here." His face was really stiff now. He was getting very mad.

"We didn't call you to fix the air lock," the man said. "We called you because one of our scientists is missing."

"Well, that's a better reason," Ted said. "But how do you know for sure that the scientist is missing?"

"Because we tried to find him when the air lock broke," the man said. "He's a computer scientist. All the air locks on New Earth are controlled by a computer. The scientist—his name's Brian Heath—made the computer. He's the only one who knows all about it. We wanted him to get the computer to fix the broken air lock. But we couldn't find him. He's missing."

"You're sure?"

"Yes," said the man. "We've looked everywhere. We don't know what's happened to him. We're worried about him. And about everyone who lives in the domes. What if another air lock breaks down? What if *all* of them break down? There'll be no one to get the computer to fix them. We'll be trapped inside the domes. We won't be able to get out. And no one will be able to get in."

"I'll try to find out where your scientist has gone," Ted said. "Where does he live? I'll go there and see what I can learn."

"I'll take you there," the man said. "You can talk to his wife."

THE MISSING SCIENTISTS

The man took Ted to the missing scientist's home. He told Heather Heath who Ted was and why he had come. Then he left. Mrs. Heath led Ted into the house. Then both of them sat down.

Ted asked, "When did you last see your husband, Mrs. Heath?"

"Two days ago," she answered. "I left the house to work in the fields outside the dome. When I came home Brian wasn't here. I talked to his friends. None of them had seen him. He wasn't at the computer center where he worked. I waited for him to come home. But he never did."

"You haven't heard from him since?"

"No, I haven't."

Ted asked, "Was your husband in any kind of trouble?"

"Not that I know of," Mrs. Heath answered. "He was everyone's friend. Everyone liked him."

Ted thought for several minutes. Then he asked, "Are any of your husband's clothes missing?"

"No," Mrs. Heath answered. "I checked. They're all there. It seems like he just walked out and disappeared into thin air."

"Would you show me where your husband keeps his clothes?"

Mrs. Heath led Ted into another room. He began to look through the clothes that belonged to Brian Heath. Suddenly he had an idea.

He turned to Mrs. Heath. "Did your husband ever leave the dome? I know he worked in the computer center inside the dome. But did he ever go outside?"

"He did leave the dome now and then," Mrs. Heath said. "He liked to walk around outside. He said he sometimes felt trapped inside the dome."

"He'd need a spacesuit outside—because of the blue gas," Ted said. "I don't see a spacesuit here. Where is it, Mrs. Heath?"

Ted could see that his question had taken Mrs. Heath by surprise. She looked through her husband's clothes. "I don't know where it is," she said. "He didn't use it very often. I didn't even know it wasn't here."

It's gone and so is your husband, Ted thought to himself. Then he thought about his ship. He wished he were back on it. He didn't want to be looking for a missing husband. The man had probably run off to some other world. Mrs. Heath had said that her husband sometimes felt trapped inside the dome. Probably he had run off to a world without domes.

Ted pushed the thoughts from his mind. "Your husband must have gone outside the dome in his spacesuit. Did anyone look for him outside?"

Mrs. Heath said, "Yes. But maybe the people who looked for him just didn't see him. Do you think we should send some people outside to look for him again?"

"Yes, I do," Ted said. He said good-bye and left the house. Then he got some people together and told them what he wanted them to do. They said they'd be glad to look outside the dome again for Brian Heath. Ted said he'd go with them.

Everyone put on spacesuits. Then they left the dome and began to look for the missing scientist. While they were looking they met some other people. Those people were carrying the dead bodies from the broken air lock back to the dome. They would take the bodies inside through an air lock that worked.

The people with Ted looked for Brian Heath for a long time. They couldn't find him. Finally Ted said, "He could be far away from here by now. Maybe he lost his way. Let's go back."

The group headed back to the dome through the blue gas. They had almost reached it when someone grabbed Ted's arm. Ted turned around. A woman held his arm. She pointed. Ted saw a man in a spacesuit walking slowly toward them.

The woman said, "That's Brian Heath! We've found him!"

"Or he's found us," Ted said. He was glad to see the missing man. Now it was all over. He could return Heath to his wife and leave New Earth. He could return to his ship—to his really important work.

The people helped Heath into the dome's air lock. After the blue gas left they all took off their spacesuits. Then they went into the dome. Ted went with them.

Inside the dome, Ted could see that something was wrong with Heath. The man just didn't look right. His eyes looked empty. He didn't seem to know where he was. He just stood inside the dome. He didn't look around. He didn't move. He seemed to be waiting for someone to tell him what to do.

"Mr. Heath," Ted said. "I'm a police officer. Where were you?"

Heath didn't even look at Ted. And he didn't answer the question. Ted took him by the arm. "Mr. Heath, what happened to you?"

"I don't know," Heath answered in a low voice.

"I'll take you home to your wife," Ted said. He led Heath away after thanking the people for their help.

All the way home, Heath said nothing. Even when Ted took him inside the house, he still said nothing.

Mrs. Heath threw her arms around her husband. She said, "I'm so glad you're safe!" The scientist just looked at her. She let him go. "Brian, don't you know me?"

Heath shook his head. Mrs. Heath looked at Ted.

"Something has happened to your husband," Ted said. "I don't know what it is. But he seems all mixed up."

"Brian," said Mrs. Heath. "One of the domes has a broken air lock. A lot of people were in it when it broke. The blue gas got into it. The people all died—all but one. We've been looking for you so you can fix it."

Heath said, "Air lock? What is an air lock?"

Mrs. Heath backed away from her husband.

Ted spoke to him. "They told me that you made the computer that controls all the air locks on New Earth. That's true, isn't it?"

"I don't remember anything about making a computer," Heath said.

His wife said, "Brian, you *did* make the computer! You're the best computer scientist in all the worlds!"

"I don't remember anything about any computer," Heath said. He sat down and dropped his head in his hands.

Just then, the telescreen rang. Mrs. Heath reached out and turned it on. A woman's face appeared on it.

"Hello, Mrs. Dexter," Mrs. Heath said. Then she listened as Mrs. Dexter asked if she had seen Mr. Dexter. Mrs. Dexter said that her husband was missing. She hadn't seen him since the day before.

"I haven't seen Sid," Mrs. Heath said. Then she told Mrs. Dexter that her husband had also disappeared two days ago. But she told Mrs. Dexter that he was back now.

Suddenly Mrs. Dexter said that she had to go. Someone was at her door. Mrs. Heath turned off the telescreen and spoke to Ted.

"Sid Dexter is a scientist. He's the man who grows all our food—and he's the only one who knows how to grow it. If he doesn't come back soon, all our food plants will die—and then so will we!"

"That makes two scientists who have disappeared," Ted said. "One's back. But one isn't. I think I'd better have a talk with Mrs. Dexter."

Mrs. Heath told Ted where the Dexters lived. On his way there he thought about his ship. He began to wonder if he'd ever get back to it.

OUTSIDE THE DOME

When Ted got to the Dexter house, he knocked on the door. Mrs. Dexter opened it.

"I'm Officer Prentiss of the Space Police," Ted told her.

Mrs. Dexter said, "Oh, I was going to call the Space Police. My husband has been missing since yesterday. But some people just found him outside the dome. They brought him home a few minutes ago."

"He's back?"

"Yes," said Mrs. Dexter. "But there's something wrong with him."

Ted asked, "What?"

"I don't really know," Mrs. Dexter answered. "But something is. He's just not himself. He seems different. I'm not sure he even knows who I am."

"I'd like to talk to your husband," Ted said.

Mrs. Dexter led him into the kitchen. Sid Dexter was standing there. He was looking out a window. He didn't turn when Ted came into the room.

"Mr. Dexter," Ted said. "Where did you go yesterday?"

Sid Dexter just shook his head.

Ted asked him, "You don't know where you went?"

Dexter shook his head again.

"Two important scientists disappear," Ted said. "Both of them return—and don't know where they've been."

Mrs. Dexter asked, "Is Brian Heath the other person you're talking about?"

Ted said, "Yes." Then he explained how Heath had walked up to him outside the dome. He said that Heath couldn't remember what had happened to him.

"Just like Sid," Mrs. Dexter said. "He seems all mixed up. He seems so strange."

Ted went over to where Sid Dexter was standing at the window. "Shouldn't you take a look at the plants you've been growing, Mr. Dexter? No one has been taking care of them while you were gone."

Dexter turned from the window. He looked at Ted. He said, "Plants? What plants?"

"Officer Prentiss is talking about the plants you grow for our food," Mrs. Dexter said to her husband. "The ones you grow in water."

He looked over at her. "I don't know anything about that," he said.

Ted asked Mrs. Dexter to come with him. Together they left the kitchen. In the next room, Ted said, "Do you have any other scientists living on New Earth?"

"Yes, we do," answered Mrs. Dexter. "There are several others." She gave Ted their names.

Ted asked her next, "Who's in charge of this world?"

Mrs. Dexter said the man in charge of New Earth was named Governor Leonard Bixby. Ted thanked her. He told her to take good care of her husband. He said he'd try to find out what had happened to him. Then he left the house.

He went at once to see Leonard Bixby. He asked Bixby if he knew that Sid Dexter and Brian Heath had disappeared and then returned.

"No, I hadn't heard that," Bixby said.

"They can't remember anything now," Ted said. "Heath says he knows nothing about air locks. But he worked on the computer that controlled them before he disappeared. Dexter says that he doesn't know anything about growing food plants in water. But that was his job before he disappeared."

"This is bad," Bixby said. "Very bad. Those two scientists are needed to keep New Earth in good order. Some of us know a little about air locks. But none of us knows very much about growing food in water. If Dexter can't remember how to do it, we'll run out of food in a very short time."

"I understand you have other scientists on your world," Ted said.

"Yes, we do."

"You'd better check on them," Ted went on.

Blue gas makes
workers dream,
page 6.

Space Police ship opens fire on C-2, page 9.

Men let blue gas enter Ted's spacesuit, page 32.

Dr. Ching Lee plants brain cells in scientists' heads, page 54.

"Why? Do you think they might disappear, too?"

"They might," Ted answered.

Bixby made several calls. He sent some people to check on the other scientists who lived on New Earth. Then he turned back to Ted. He asked, "Is there anything more I should do?"

"I have an idea," Ted said. He told his idea to Bixby.

"That's very interesting," Bixby said when Ted had finished explaining his idea. "I'd say it's worth trying."

Mr. Bixby started helping Ted put his idea to work. He found Ted a place to live. He got him some clothes. Then he told everyone that Ted was a scientist. But some people had talked with Ted when he first got to New Earth. They knew he was a police officer. So Bixby told them to go along with the story that Ted was a scientist. He told them to say that Ted knew how to destroy the blue gas that covered the world outside the domes.

The people of New Earth helped Bixby and Ted. They sent word to other worlds about the new scientist who had come to New Earth.

Then Ted waited to see if his plan would work. He believed that someone must have done something to Heath and Dexter. There was no other way to explain the way they had changed. But he didn't know if he was right. That's why he had decided to say he was a scientist who had come to work on New Earth. If someone was doing something to the scientists of New Earth, that person might try to do the same thing to Ted.

So he waited. A day passed. Nothing happened. But the next day he received a message on the computer.

The message said that Ted must come outside the dome in two hours. There he would be met by the person who had sent the message. That person would give him important facts he needed to know about the blue gas. Until then Ted was not to try to destroy the blue gas. If he did, New Earth would be in trouble.

Ted couldn't sit still while he waited for the time to pass. He got up and walked around. Then he sat down. Then he got up and walked around some more.

Finally it was time for him to go. He got his laser gun and put it under his clothes. He smiled to himself. No one would think that a scientist would have a laser gun hidden under his clothes.

He went to the nearest air lock. He picked up his spacesuit where he had left it. Then he put it on and stepped inside. The door closed. Then the second door opened and he walked outside. He went to the place the message had told him to go.

When he got there, he saw no one. He began to wonder if the message had been a trick. He walked around. Then he heard a noise. He turned around quickly. A man in a spacesuit stood near by.

Ted could see only the man's face. It was very white. The man's eyes were very black. Ted didn't like the look in the man's eyes. They looked wild, he thought.

He began to walk toward the man. The black eyes seemed to draw him on. Then the man held up his right hand. Ted stopped walking and started to speak. Just then someone grabbed him from behind.

Ted tried as hard as he could to break free. He put up a good fight. But it was no use. He couldn't get away.

The man with the black eyes came up to him. He reached out. He opened the part of Ted's spacesuit that covered his head. The blue gas quickly filled Ted's nose. Suddenly he saw his fleet commander standing near by.

"I don't want you in the Space Police," she said. "You're not a good officer, Prentiss!"

DR. CHING LEE SHOWS UP

"I *am* a good police officer!" Ted heard himself shout at his fleet commander. "I am!"

"You're not," said the fleet commander. "You only want to do the police work that *you* want to do. You think you can decide what police work is important and what isn't."

Ted shouted, "That's not true!" But he knew that it was true.

"*All* police work is important," said the fleet commander. "I don't want officers working with me who don't think that."

"Listen," Ted said. "I'm sorry about what happened before—when you told me to come here to New Earth. I didn't want to come. But I did. I found out that there's big trouble here. This job *is* important. I know that now."

The man with the black eyes laughed at Ted. The fleet commander just looked at him. Then the fleet commander disappeared. Suddenly Ted felt himself lifted off the ground.

Someone carried Ted through the blue gas. He couldn't get free. The domes moved far away. Then Ted saw a spaceship on the ground in front of him.

Ted was carried on board the spaceship. Then he was put down. He turned to face the person who had been carrying him. It was a big man. He looked like a giant.

Ted didn't waste a minute. He hit the big man as hard as he could. The man just laughed. Ted hit him again. The man laughed even louder. He wasn't hurt a bit.

Then the black-eyed man appeared. He gave the big man an order. The big man grabbed Ted again. He pulled off Ted's spacesuit and threw it on the floor. Then he picked Ted up and carried him toward a door. The man with the black eyes opened the door. The big man threw

Ted into the room behind it. Then he closed the door and locked it from the outside.

There was only a little light in the room. Ted could hardly see. But he looked around. The room was empty. There were no chairs or tables. Not even a window. Ted couldn't tell where the light came from.

He sat down on the hard floor. He didn't feel very well. His head felt funny. He couldn't seem to get his thoughts together. He shook his head from side to side. It began to clear.

He thought about what had just happened to him. He knew the two men outside must be the ones who had done something to Heath and Dexter. But there was one thing he couldn't understand at all. What was his fleet commander doing here on New Earth?

Then it hit him. *The blue gas!* His fleet commander hadn't been there at all. Ted had only thought she was. And because he had thought so, the blue gas had made his thoughts take real shape.

Ted had been worried since he had come to New Earth. He had been worried because he hadn't said yes right away to the orders his fleet commander had given him. He had been wrong to do that. He knew that now. He had thought the trouble on New Earth wasn't important. Now he knew that it was. The fleet commander had been right. All police work was important.

At the time he had tried to get out of going to New Earth. Now he was afraid that he would be forced to leave the Space Police. Ted saw what he had been thinking. The fleet commander had appeared to kick him out of the Space Police.

Ted made up his mind to try as hard as he could to say yes to orders right away. Then maybe the fleet commander would forget that Ted had tried to get out of coming to New Earth.

Ted got up. He walked around the room. He pounded on the walls. They were very strong. He knew he couldn't break them down. Then he tried to open the door. It didn't move.

He sat down on the floor again. He decided there was nothing he could do. The next move was up to the man with the black eyes. He wondered what that move would be. He was sure he wouldn't like it.

Time passed. Ted tried once more to open the door. He couldn't. Then he listened for sounds. For a long time he heard none. But then he did hear a sound. It came from a long way off. It was weak. Ted wasn't sure what the sound was.

He listened closely. Then he knew. It was the sound of people walking. The sound came closer. Then he heard someone at the door.

He got ready. When the door opened he would fight his way out. He watched the door. It began to move. He grabbed it. He pulled it all the way open.

Behind it was the big man. Ted tried to jump him. But the man sent Ted flying back into the room. He banged his head against the room's far wall. The blow knocked him out.

Some time later he woke up. He didn't know how long he'd been out. When he opened his eyes he found that he was still in the same room. But someone was there with him. Beside him sat a woman. She had long black hair and dark eyes behind her round glasses. When the woman saw that Ted's eyes were open she spoke to him.

"How do you feel?"

"Like my head is about to fall off," he answered. "Who are you? How did you get here?"

"My name is Ching Lee," the woman said. "I'm from New Earth. I know you. You're the new scientist everyone's talking about."

"I'm not a scientist," Ted said. "That was only a story I asked Mr. Bixby to tell everyone."

Ching asked, "Why did you do that? Who are you really?"

"I did it to see if I could find out what happened to the two scientists who disappeared. I'm really an officer of the Space Police. My name's Ted Prentiss."

"I didn't know any of our scientists had disappeared," Ching said.

Ted told her what had happened to Brian Heath and Sid Dexter and how mixed up they seemed when they returned. He also told her about the message he had received. He explained that he had come outside the dome to meet the person who had sent him the message. He told Ching what had happened to him when he met the man with the black eyes.

Ching said, "The same thing happened to me! I also got a message. It said that someone had important facts about my work—facts I should know. So I came outside the dome."

"And you met the man with the black eyes?"

"Yes," she said. "I did. He pulled off the part of my spacesuit that covers my face. The blue gas made me see things that weren't really there. Then a giant of a man brought me here."

Ted asked, "Are you a scientist?"

"I'm a doctor," Ching said. "I was working on a way to stop the blue gas from hurting the people of New Earth."

"And now you're here," Ted said. "Just like me. And just like Brian Heath and Sid Dexter probably were. But *why* are we here? That's the big question."

"Maybe the man with the black eyes doesn't like scientists," Ching said.

As she spoke, the door opened. The man with the black eyes came into the room.

"It's not that I don't like scientists. I'm one myself," he said. "It's something more than that."

Ted asked, "What is it?"

"Come with me," the man told him. "I'll tell you. You'll both want to know. Because what happened to Heath and Dexter is about to happen to you. Of course you won't remember any of it when it's all over."

Then the big man came into the room. He forced Ted and Ching to follow the man with the black eyes.

THE MIND THIEF

Ted and Ching were taken into a big room.

"This is my laboratory," the man with the black eyes told them. "This is where I do my work."

Ching asked him, "Just who are you?" His spacesuit was off now and she could see him well.

"My name is Alex Brent."

"Dr. Brent!" said Ching. "I've heard about you. And I've seen pictures of you. You used to live and work on New Earth."

"Yes, I did."

Ching went on. "The people of New Earth made you leave their world. They found out what you were doing."

Ted asked, "What was that?"

"I was experimenting on the human brain," the doctor answered.

"He was supposed to be working on a way to keep the blue gas from hurting the people of New Earth," Ching said. "But he experimented on people's brains instead. Some of the people died. That's why the other people made him leave New Earth. Then they asked me to try to do something about the blue gas."

"The people of New Earth are behind the times," said Dr. Brent. His black eyes flashed. "I could have opened up new worlds to them. Worlds of the human mind. But no. They said I was doing wrong."

"You were," said Ching. "You were killing people with your experiments."

"They had to die to help science move forward," Dr. Brent said.

Ted asked, "What did you do to Heath and Dexter?"

"The same thing I'm going to do to the two of you. I've found a way to take a person's knowledge from the brain," said Dr. Brent.

"So that's why Heath and Dexter can't remember anything about the work they used to do," Ted said.

"Right," said Dr. Brent. He no longer smiled. "I took Heath's knowledge of the computer that controls the air locks on New Earth. I also took Dexter's knowledge of how to grow food in water."

Ching asked, "Why did you do it?"

"I did it because of what the people of New Earth did to me. I wanted to get even with them for making me leave. And I will. I'm going to take away the knowledge of all their scientists. I've passed a death sentence on New Earth. Yes, a death sentence. Without their scientists' knowledge, New Earth will break down and die."

Dr. Brent went to the other side of his laboratory. He picked up two red bottles.

"Any doctor can take brain cells from a person," he said. "But no doctor knows how to keep those brain cells alive for more than a few minutes. No doctor but me, that is. I know how to keep brain cells alive for a very long time. I'm keeping alive the brain cells in these two bottles. They're the ones I took from Heath and Dexter."

Ching looked at Ted. Then she turned back to Dr. Brent. "You plan to take my brain cells, too," she said. "You want to take my knowledge of the blue gas."

"That's right," said Dr. Brent. "I want the blue gas to stay just the way it is. I want it that way so it will kill the people of New Earth."

Ching said, "I won't let you take my brain cells!"

"You have nothing to say about it," said Dr. Brent. "You can't stop me."

"You've made a mistake, you know," Ted said.

Dr. Brent put down the two red bottles. "What do you mean? What mistake did I make?"

"I'm not a scientist," Ted told him. "I'm an officer in the Space Police. I have no knowledge that you can use to hurt New Earth."

"But everyone said you were a scientist," Dr. Brent said.

"We told that story in the hope that you would get in touch with me," Ted said. "And you fell for it. You did get in touch with me. But I know nothing that can help you destroy New Earth."

"I don't believe you," Dr. Brent said.

Ted showed him his badge. Dr. Brent looked down at it as he took it in his hand. Ted pulled his laser gun out from under his clothes.

"Now it's my show," he said. "Don't move, Brent. And tell your man behind us to join you over there."

Dr. Brent dropped Ted's badge to the floor. He spoke to the big man who was standing behind Ted and Ching. As the man walked behind Ted and Ching, he grabbed Ted around the neck. Ted's laser gun fell from his hand. The big man picked it up and let go of Ted.

"Good work," Dr. Brent said to his helper. "Our young Space Police officer isn't as smart as he thinks he is."

Ching put her hand on Ted's arm.

"Well, now," said Dr. Brent. "What shall we do with our brave officer? Since he's not a scientist, I really have no use for his brain cells. On the other hand, I can't just let him go. That would be a mistake."

The big man said two words: "Kill him."

"Yes, I could do that," Dr. Brent went on. "It would be very easy. But I don't think I will."

Ted kept his eyes on the doctor. He waited to hear what the man would say.

Dr. Brent spoke again. "I think I'll take our young officer's knowledge from his brain after all. It's of no use to me. But it will be a good way to pay him back for the trick he played on me. Yes. That's what I'll do."

Dr. Brent spoke to the big man. The man gave the doctor Ted's laser gun. Then he went after Ted. Ted tried to fight him off. But he was too weak. The man picked him up and carried him across the room. He put him on a table. Then he tied him to the table.

"Very good," said Dr. Brent. "Now I'm ready to begin." He handed Ted's gun back to the big man. "Watch the woman," he said.

The big man crossed the room. He stood next to Ching. He pointed the gun at her. She didn't say a word. She didn't move.

Suddenly she gave a loud shout. The sudden shout scared the big man. He jumped back. Ching kicked his hand—the hand that held Ted's gun. The gun flew out of the man's hand.

Ching dropped to the floor where the gun had fallen. She grabbed the gun. "Set Ted free!" she ordered.

The big man didn't move. Dr. Brent didn't move either.

Ching shouted, "Do as I say! I'll shoot if I have to."

Dr. Brent began to free Ted. In a few seconds the ropes were off. Ted jumped down from the table. He joined Ching. She gave him his laser gun.

Ted looked at Ching. He asked, "Can you put the brain cells that Brent took from Heath and Dexter back into their brains?"

"Yes, I can," Ching said. "I can inject the cells into their brains. Then they'll remember everything again. Let's hurry. I'll get the two red bottles."

When Ching had the bottles, Ted spoke to Dr. Brent and his helper. "You two are coming with us. Let's go!"

The big man started for the door of the laboratory. He went outside. Dr. Brent began to follow him. But just as Brent was about to go out the door he turned around fast. He grabbed Ching and took the bottles from her hands.

Then he pushed her out of the laboratory door.

Ted made a grab for Brent. But the doctor gave him a push that sent him flying out of the laboratory. Then Dr. Brent closed the door and locked himself inside.

Ted started to stand up in the hall outside the laboratory. The big man jumped him. Ted fired one shot. It hit the big man. He fell to the floor. A minute later he was dead.

"Now we've got to get Brent," Ted said. He tried to push open the laboratory door. "No good," he said. "I'll have to shoot it open."

He fired at the door. It blew open. Dr. Brent stood in the center of his laboratory.

"I'll shoot you if you give us any more trouble," Ted told him.

"No you won't," said Dr. Brent.

"I told you I'll shoot you if I have to," Ted said.

"Let me tell you something," Dr. Brent said. "If you kill me you'll destroy the knowledge I took from Heath and Dexter."

Ted asked, "What do you mean by that? Where are the two red bottles?"

"While you shot my helper, I injected Heath's and Dexter's brain cells into my own brain. If you kill me now their knowledge will die with me."

Ching turned to whisper in Ted's ear. "The brain cells live for a short time after a person dies."

Ted looked at her. Then he said, "Let's take this man to the hospital—right away."

BRAIN CELLS

Ted looked at Dr. Brent. "OK," he said. "I won't kill you. But I am going to take you back to the domes with me. You have Heath's and Dexter's brain cells in your own brain. That means you know how to fix broken air locks and grow food in water. The people of New Earth won't die now with you to help them."

"I won't help those people," Dr. Brent said. "I'd rather die first."

Ching asked Ted, "How can we make him do it?"

He didn't answer her. Instead he moved slowly across the room toward Dr. Brent.

"Stay away from me," Dr. Brent said. He backed away from Ted. But Ted kept coming. When he got close to Brent he handed his gun to Ching. Then he quickly reached out and grabbed the doctor around the neck. Dr. Brent tried to break free. But Ted held on to him. Then he pressed a place on the side of Dr. Brent's neck. He pressed it as hard as he could.

In less than a minute Dr. Brent's eyes closed. He would have slipped to the floor if Ted hadn't held on to him.

"He's out cold," Ted said to Ching. "I'll carry him back to the domes. But we need to find three spacesuits first. We'll each need one. And Dr. Brent will need one too. We don't want that blue gas to get us on our way back."

"I'll look for my suit," Ching said. "They made me take it off when they brought me here."

"Mine must be here, too," Ted said. "That big man pulled it off me when I came on board. See if you can find it. And Brent's suit must be nearby, too."

Ching put down the gun and went to look for the spacesuits. It didn't take her long to find them. She brought them back to the laboratory and helped Ted put one on Dr. Brent. Then she and Ted put on their suits.

Ted lifted Dr. Brent and headed toward the domes. Ching picked up the gun and followed him. Finally they saw the domes in front of them. They went into the nearest one.

As soon as they got inside they took off their spacesuits. Then they took off Dr. Brent's suit.

Ching asked Ted, "Now what?"

"First let me have the gun. Then let's find the hospital," he said.

"I work there," Ching said. "I'll show you where it is."

Ted picked up Dr. Brent again. Then he followed Ching into another dome. He could see the hospital. But as they walked toward it Dr. Brent woke up. Ted didn't know that he was awake. Ching was in front of Ted. She didn't know either.

Suddenly Dr. Brent hit Ted on the side of his head. Ted fell to the floor. Dr. Brent fell next to him. But then he jumped up. Quickly he looked through Ted's clothes. He found what he was looking for—the laser gun.

"I told you I wouldn't help the people of New Earth," he said. "I *never* will. Now I'm going to fix you once and for all. You've given me too much trouble."

The sound of the fall had made Ching turn around and run toward Ted.

She shouted, "Ted, look out!"

Dr. Brent fired a shot at Ted. But the shot missed. Before he could fire again Ching kicked the gun from his hand. Then she picked it up before Dr. Brent could get it again.

Brent started to go for her. She fired Ted's gun at him. Her shot caught him in the chest. He stopped in his tracks. There was a surprised look on his face.

Brent looked down at his chest. Blood was escaping from it. He looked up at Ching. He tried to say something but no words came from his mouth. Then he fell to the ground.

Ted said, "Oh, no! You've killed him! Now we'll never be able to help Heath and Dexter. Their brain cells were injected into Brent's brain. Now they'll die with him."

"You're wrong," Ching said. "Dr. Brent is dead. But his brain isn't. We have three or four minutes. If we move fast we can save those brain cells."

Ted picked up Dr. Brent. He and Ching ran into the hospital. Then Ching went right to work on Dr. Brent's brain. She used a long needle to take cells from Dr. Brent's brain. She put the cells into a special liquid.

"Now we've got to get Heath and Dexter to come here," she said. "This liquid will keep the brain cells alive for a few more minutes. When Heath and Dexter get here I'll inject the cells into their brains."

Ted ran from the hospital. He found Heath first. Then he found Dexter. The three men ran to the hospital.

Ching Lee was waiting for them. She went right to work on Brian Heath. She used her long needle to inject half of the brain cells into his brain. Then she injected the other half into Sid Dexter's brain. Both men seemed to wake up out of a dream. Their faces changed. Their eyes grew brighter than they had been before.

Brian Heath asked what had happened to him. Ted told him.

"Then I'd better get busy," Heath said. "I'll go to the computer at once and get it to fix the broken air lock." He left the hospital.

"I'd better go, too," Dexter said. "I've got to check on the food I was growing. If I don't get there fast, a lot of the plants will die."

When Dexter had gone, Ted turned to Ching. "Thanks for all you've done," he said to her. "I never would have made it without your help. You saved my life. And you've helped the people of New Earth stay alive."

"I'm only sorry about one thing," Ching said.

"What's that?"

"I'm sorry that I had to kill Dr. Brent. As a doctor, I try to save lives. Not destroy them."

"You had to do it," Ted told her. "You couldn't help it."

He looked around the hospital. Everything was quiet.

"I'll be leaving New Earth now," Ted said. "It's time to get back to my ship."

"Good-bye," Ching Lee said. "And thanks for helping us."

Ted started toward his capsule. On the way he ran into Brian Heath. Heath had a strange look on his face. He said, "I got the computer to fix the broken air lock. So that's all set. But there's something funny about my mind since Dr. Lee injected those cells into it."

Ted asked, "What's funny?"

"I know things now that I didn't know before," Heath said. "And I talked to Sid Dexter. He knows new things now, too."

Ted asked Heath, "What do you two know now that you didn't know before?"

"For one thing, Sid knows some facts about computer science that he never knew before. And I know things about growing food."

Ted asked, "Anything else?"

"We both know a little more about keeping a person's brain cells alive for a long time. Together we know how to do the whole thing. Only Dr. Brent knew how to do that. And he's dead. It sure is strange, what's happened to me and Sid."

Ted said, "It's *great!* Don't you see? Ching Lee must have given each of you some of Dr. Brent's brain cells when she gave you back your own. Now you and Sid can teach Ching Lee how to keep brain cells alive for a long time. She can take brain cells from every person who dies here on New Earth. Then she can inject them into a living person. That way none of the knowledge on New Earth will ever be lost!"

"I hadn't thought of that," Heath said. "But you're right. Sid and I will teach Dr. Lee how to do it. Soon New Earth will have the smartest people of any world in space."

"Thanks to Dr. Brent," Ted said. "I wonder what he'd say if he knew how things have turned out."

"I don't think he would be very happy," Heath said.

"I'm sure he wouldn't," Ted said. He laughed. "Brent wanted to destroy New Earth. But by dying he's made it better than ever."

Ted said good-bye to Heath. Then he walked to the air lock and put on his spacesuit. When the door opened he went to his capsule. He got inside and set its controls. Then the capsule shot up into space.

Soon Ted was back on his ship—and happy.

As soon as he could he got in touch with the fleet commander. He told the woman everything that had happened on New Earth.

"You did a fine job," the fleet commander said. "The people on New Earth would have died if you hadn't helped them. And since you did such good work, I'm sending you out on another job. It's on a world not far from here. The people there called us and asked us to send them our best officer. It seems that something strange is happening to their children."

Ted said, "Oh, no!"

The fleet commander barked, "What did you say, Prentiss?"

Ted had learned his lesson. He wasn't going to try to turn down this new job. He knew the fleet commander was right—all police work was important. The problem with the children on that other world would turn out to be important, too.

The fleet commander shouted again, "I asked you what you said, Prentiss!"

"I said I can't wait to go," Ted told her.

And soon he was on his way to another world and another Space Police job.